KIRILL KAPRIZOV

HOCKEY SUPERSTAR

BY ROY RATHBURN

Book design by Jake Nordby
Cover design by Jake Nordby

Photographs ©: Matt Krohn/AP Images, cover, 1; Harry How/Getty Images Sport/Getty Images, 4–5, 6; Claus Andersen/Getty Images Sport/Getty Images, 8; Maksim Bogodvid/Sputnik/AP Images, 11; Vladimir Fedorenko/Sputnik/AP Images, 13, 17; Alexander Vilf/Sputnik/AP Images, 14; Jean Catuffe/Getty Images Sport/Getty Images, 18; Stacy Bengs/AP Images, 20–21, 30; Chris Tanouye/Freestyle Photography/Getty Images Sport/Getty Images, 22–23; Mitchell Leff/ Getty Images Sport/Getty Images, 25; David Berding/Getty Images Sport/Getty Images, 26–27; Red Line Editorial, 29

Press Box Books, an imprint of Press Room Editions, Inc.

ISBN
978-1-63494-873-9 (library bound)
978-1-63494-891-3 (paperback)
978-1-63494-925-5 (epub)
978-1-63494-909-5 (hosted ebook)

Library of Congress Control Number: 2023922763

Distributed by North Star Editions, Inc.
2297 Waters Drive
Mendota Heights, MN 55120
www.northstareditions.com

Printed in the United States of America
082024

About the Author

Roy Rathburn is a retired English teacher and former hockey player, coach, and official, from northern Minnesota.

TABLE OF CONTENTS

97
BAUER
MINNESOTA WILD
KAPRIZOV

1 WORTH THE WAIT

Kirill Kaprizov was looking for an opportunity in overtime. And it wasn't long before he found one. The young left winger gained control of the puck after pouncing on a bad pass. In an instant, the rookie raced toward the goal.

Minnesota Wild fans watching at home were on the edge of their seats. They had waited more than five years for Kaprizov to make his National Hockey League (NHL) debut. So far, he was everything they'd hoped for. Kaprizov had already picked up

Kirill Kaprizov led all rookies in scoring in the 2020–21 season with 51 points.

Kaprizov (center) receives a hug after scoring the overtime winner in his NHL debut.

assists on two of the Wild's three goals against the Los Angeles Kings.

Wild fans weren't the only ones watching closely. Kaprizov's fans, friends, and family were watching back home in Russia. Kaprizov had played in his home country since the Wild drafted him in 2015. Now, they hoped to see him succeed in the NHL.

Kaprizov was too fast for the Kings defenders to catch him. He skated at full speed toward the goalie. Then he slammed on the brakes just inches from the netminder's face. Kaprizov poked the puck between the goalie's open leg pads for the game-winning goal.

The entire Wild team poured off the bench in celebration. They were excited for Kaprizov's first NHL goal. More importantly, the team was celebrating a season-opening win. Kaprizov became just the third player ever to score an overtime winner in his NHL debut. Wild fans hoped there would be many more goals to come.

A DELAYED START

Kirill Kaprizov officially joined the Wild for the start of the 2020–21 season. However, due to the COVID-19 pandemic, the season didn't begin until January 2021. Kaprizov's final game in Russia took place in March 2020. That meant he went 10 months without playing in a game.

ALROSA
ALROSA
ALROSA
CCM
NEXUS
BAUER

2 HOMETOWN HERO

Kirill Kaprizov was born on April 26, 1997, in Novokuznetsk, Russia. Kirill's family lived about 40 miles (64 km) away in a small village. Kirill started playing hockey when he was four. Every day, he and his brother made the trip into the city for practice.

As Kirill got older, his hockey skills quickly improved. So, his family decided to move to Novokuznetsk. Kirill's coaches were amazed at his talent. And his teammates looked up to him as a leader.

Kirill Kaprizov first played for the Russian junior national hockey team in 2014.

Kirill took practice seriously and worked hard to get better.

For most players, moving up from youth hockey to junior hockey is difficult. But Kirill found it easy. He nearly skipped juniors entirely. However, he was too young to turn pro. So, Kirill played just one season of juniors. Then, at the age of 17, he joined Russia's top pro league.

Russia's league is called the Kontinental Hockey League (KHL). Many hockey experts consider it the best league in the world after the NHL. It attracts players from

KIRILL OFF THE ICE

Hockey keeps Kirill Kaprizov very busy. But in his free time, he enjoys playing video games such as *Counter-Strike* and *Dota*. He also likes to go back to Russia during the off-season. There he enjoys fishing and spending time with family.

Kirill Kaprizov became one of the most popular players in the KHL when he played in the league.

ХОККЕЙНАЯ ЛИГА

all over the globe. But fans especially love their Russian stars. Kirill stayed at home to play for Novokuznetsk. Fans and teammates adored the hometown prodigy.

Kirill was much younger than most players in the league. And early on, he struggled to adapt to the KHL. In his first 31 games, he scored only four goals. Those numbers didn't get him noticed by NHL scouts. Few NHL teams were even aware of Kirill at all. In fact, it took a total accident for a Minnesota Wild scout to see Kirill play in his rookie KHL season.

The scout was based near Novokuznetsk. One day, his flight was canceled. The scout had some spare time in the city, so he went to a Novokuznetsk game. He noticed Kirill's ability right away. After the season, the Wild chose him in the fifth round of the NHL Entry Draft.

Teammates surround Kirill Kaprizov (17) to celebrate a goal in a 2016 KHL game.

Kirill didn't expect to be drafted. He heard the news one night while getting ready for bed. In an instant, he had a new destination. But Kirill wasn't sure if he wanted to leave his home country.

97
СОГАЗ

3 RUSSIAN ICON

Most fifth-round draft picks do not make an impact in the NHL. But Kirill Kaprizov was no ordinary fifth-rounder. The Wild felt he had the talent of a second-rounder. However, Kaprizov was still young. And the Wild didn't know if he even wanted to play in the NHL. Some Russian players enjoy being stars in the KHL. The Wild didn't want to waste a high draft pick on a player that had no interest in playing for them.

Kaprizov tallied 40 points in 46 games during his first season with CSKA Moscow.

Kaprizov was still growing as a player. Even if he wanted to play in the NHL, he needed time to improve. He increased his scoring output each year. Wild fans excitedly watched highlights of his amazing stickhandling and skating. As a 19-year-old, he scored 20 goals and added 22 assists.

The next year, he signed with CSKA Moscow, the top team in Russian hockey. In 2018, Kaprizov got an even bigger honor. Russia chose him to play for the national team in the Winter Olympics.

LEARNING MINNESOTA

Kirill Kaprizov knew nothing about Minnesota when the Wild drafted him. But he had a Novokuznetsk teammate who knew all about the place. Ryan Stoa grew up in Minnesota and played college hockey there. He told Kaprizov all about his home state. Stoa also helped Kaprizov learn some English.

Kaprizov scored 113 goals in six KHL seasons.

BAUER
97
KAZAN
33

Kaprizov (77) celebrates with a teammate after winning Olympic gold.

At 20, Kaprizov was the youngest player on the team. His lack of experience didn't slow him down, though. His five goals were tied for the most in the tournament. And he showed up on the biggest stage. In the gold-medal game, Russia trailed Germany with less than a minute to play. Kaprizov assisted the game-tying goal. Then he blasted a one-timer in overtime to win gold for his country.

Kaprizov returned to the KHL and got even better. In the 2018–19 season, he set new career highs with 30 goals and 51 total points. He also led CSKA to the league championship. At that point, Kaprizov was one of the biggest stars in the league.

Kaprizov went into the 2019–20 season on the last year of his KHL contract. Once again, he set new career highs in scoring. By this point, it had been five years since the Wild drafted him. Fans in Minnesota worried that he might just stay in Russia for good.

97
BAUER
97
BAUER
bauer
bauer

4 GOING WILD

A dream came true for Wild fans in the summer of 2020. Kirill Kaprizov decided to leave Russia. He wanted to challenge himself in the NHL.

Any team could use a player like Kaprizov. But Wild fans were especially excited. The team hadn't had many superstars in its short history. And it had never played for a Stanley Cup.

Kaprizov electrified fans right away with his overtime goal to open the 2020–21 season. By April, he had scored more

Three of Kaprizov's 27 goals in his rookie year were game-winning goals.

points than any rookie in Wild history. Not surprisingly, Kaprizov won the Calder Trophy as the NHL's Rookie of the Year.

Any worry about Kaprizov returning to Russia went away when he signed a new five-year contract with the Wild. Kaprizov played even better in his second NHL season. He smashed team records for goals, assists, and total points in a season. He also made his first All-Star Game.

In 2021–22, Kaprizov led the Wild to 53 wins.

GONE FISHIN'

Kirill Kaprizov did not hang around long after his rookie season in the NHL. He went home to Russia for some much-needed rest. He even missed the announcement that he had won the Calder Trophy. Kaprizov was fishing at the time. He didn't have access to the internet. When Kaprizov returned, he had many messages of congratulations.

After recording 51 points as a rookie, Kaprizov tallied 108 in his second season.

97
TRIA

Minnesota had never won that many games in a season. The Wild rolled into the playoffs hoping for a deep run. Kaprizov dazzled fans by notching the first playoff hat trick in team history. He went on to score seven goals in six games. However, the St. Louis Blues eliminated Minnesota in the first round.

In 2022–23, Kaprizov dealt with injuries for the first time in his young career. He missed 13 games in a crucial stretch in March and April. Despite those challenges, Kaprizov recorded 40 goals for the second year in a row. However, the goals dried up in the playoffs. Kaprizov scored just once as Minnesota suffered another first-round exit.

Kaprizov quickly became Minnesota's most important player. By his fourth season, he was already climbing the team's all-time

Kaprizov scored 114 goals in his first three NHL seasons. That put him sixth in Wild history for goals scored.

leaderboards. If he could bring a Stanley Cup to Minnesota, he would cement his legendary status among Wild fans.

HAT TRICK HISTORY

Kaprizov made history in 2022 with the first playoff hat trick ever for the Wild. On Kaprizov's first goal, he camped on the side of the net. Kaprizov whacked a rebound off the Blues goalie and into the net.

SAAD
20
HUSSO
35
97

TIMELINE

1. **Novokuznetsk, Russia (April 26, 1997)**
   Kirill Kaprizov is born.

2. **Novokuznetsk, Russia (2014)**
   Kaprizov makes his professional debut at the age of 17 with his hometown Metallurg Novokuznetsk of the Kontinental Hockey League (KHL).

3. **Sunrise, Florida (June 27, 2015)**
   The Minnesota Wild select Kaprizov in the fifth round of the 2015 NHL Entry Draft.

4. **Moscow, Russia (August 10, 2017)**
   Kaprizov signs a three-year deal with CSKA Moscow, one of the best teams in the KHL.

5. **Gangneung, South Korea (February 25, 2018)**
   Kaprizov scores the game-winning goal in overtime to win the gold medal for Russia at the Winter Olympics.

6. **Saint Paul, Minnesota (July 13, 2020)**
   After leading the KHL in goals for the second consecutive year, Kaprizov signs a two-year contract to play in the NHL for the Wild.

7. **Los Angeles, California (January 14, 2021)**
   Kaprizov makes a memorable NHL debut when he scores the game-winner in overtime for his first NHL goal.

8. **Raleigh, North Carolina (April 2, 2022)**
   Kaprizov scores his 85th point of the season to break the Wild's single-season record.

MAP

4
1
2
5
6
8
7
N
3

AT A GLANCE

Birth date: April 26, 1997

Birthplace: Novokuznetsk, Russia

Position: Left wing

Shoots: Left

Size: 5-foot-10 (178 cm), 202 pounds (92 kg)

NHL team: Minnesota Wild (2020–)

Previous teams: Metallurg Novokuznetsk (2014–16), Salavat Yulaev Ufa (2016–17), CSKA Moscow (2017–20)

Major awards: Olympic gold medal (2018), Calder Memorial Trophy (2021), NHL All-Star (2022–23)

Accurate through the 2022–23 season.

GLOSSARY

assists
Passes, rebounds, or deflections that result in goals.

contract
A written agreement that keeps a player with a team for a certain amount of time.

debut
First appearance.

draft
An event that allows teams to choose new players coming into the league.

hat trick
When a player scores three or more goals in a game.

junior hockey
A level of hockey in which young players can improve their skills.

one-timer
A shot that a player takes directly from a pass without controlling the puck first.

playoffs
A set of games to decide a league's champion.

prodigy
A young person who is extremely talented.

rookie
A first-year player.

TO LEARN MORE

Books

Berglund, Bruce. *Hockey GOATs: The Greatest Athletes of All Time*. North Mankato, MN: Capstone Press, 2024.

McDougall, Chrös. *Minnesota Wild*. Mendota Heights, MN: Press Room Editions, 2023.

Wiseman, Blaine. *Stanley Cup*. New York: Lightbox Learning, 2024.

More Information

To learn more about Kirill Kaprizov, go to **pressboxbooks.com/AllAccess**.

These links are routinely monitored and updated to provide the most current information available.

INDEX